RAPS AND RHYMES TO SAVE THE GALAXY

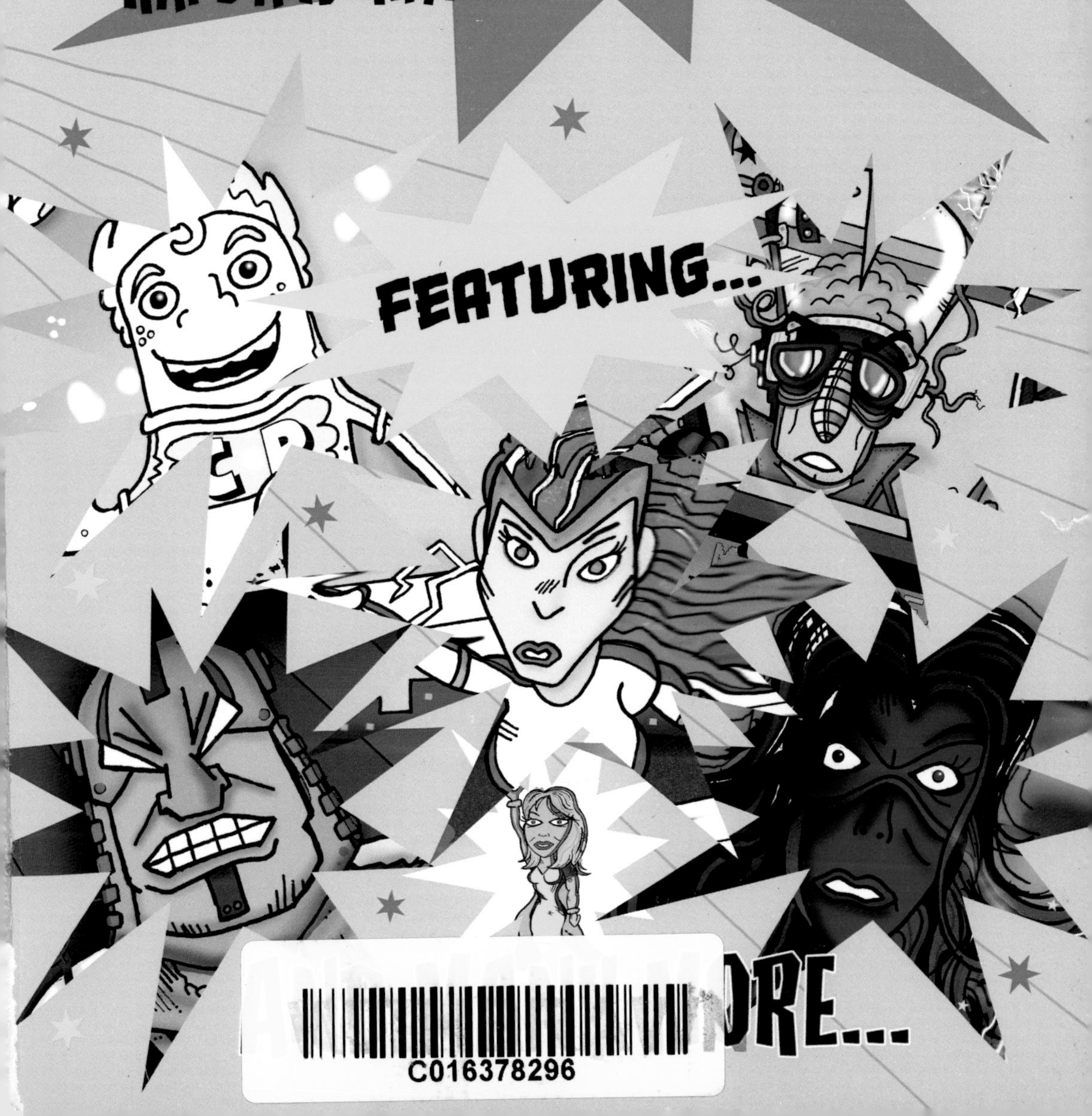
FEATURING...
ORE...

Published by TROIKA BOOKS

First published 2017

Troika Books
Well House, Green Lane, Ardleigh CO7 7PD
www.troikabooks.com

Text copyright © Neal Zetter 2017
Illustrations copyright © Chris White 2017

A CIP catalogue record for this book is available from the British Library

ISBN 978-1-909991-46-0

1 2 3 4 5 6 7 8 9 10

Printed in Poland

Contents

THE METAL MAN

THE METAL MAN DATA FILE

Secret ID – None

Top Power – Unbreakability

Place or Planet of Origin – Mac's Scrapyard, Manchester

Deadliest Enemy – The Rust Giant

Other Stuff – Has yearly services at his local garage

THE METAL MAN

I'm a man made of metal **I'm the Metal Man**
I've lived like this since I began
Made from recycled bike frames, crushed cars and tin cans
I'm a man made of metal **I'm the Metal Man**

Bits of me are copper, bits of me are steel
My feet have been constructed from two old iron wheels
People touch me and tap me to see if I'm real
But I don't let it bother me 'cause I know that I am
I'm a man made of metal **I'm the Metal Man**

Factory floor shavings were used for my hair
You're oval and round I'm rectangular and square
I don't rust in the rain 'cause I drink plenty of oil
If you peer into my brain you'll find it full of springs and coils
To keep my mind thinking
When I swim or take a bath
I'm forever sinking
If you see me drowning please stretch out your hand
I'm a man made of metal
I'm the Metal Man

I'm no ordinary bloke, wrapped in my strange, smooth, shiny skin
Though villains try to beat me I'm too tough for them to win
I don't eat or sleep
You'll never see me cry
And I can't ever die
Why?
By now I think you understand
I'm a man made of metal
I'm the Metal Man

I'm a man made of metal
I'm the Metal Man

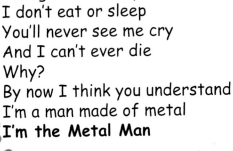

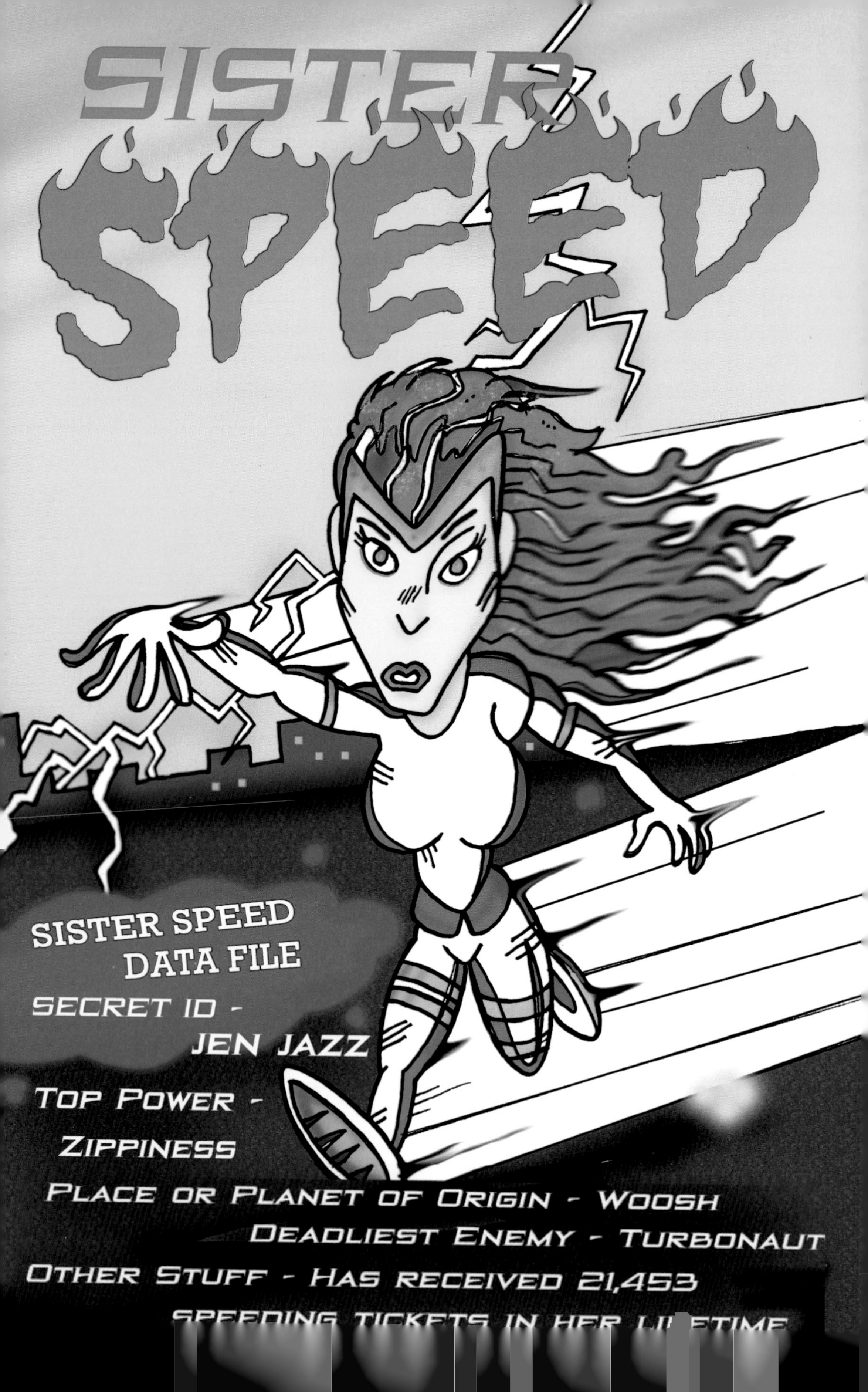
SISTER
SPEED
SISTER SPEED
DATA FILE
SECRET ID -
JEN JAZZ
TOP POWER -
ZIPPINESS
PLACE OR PLANET OF ORIGIN - WOOSH
DEADLIEST ENEMY - TURBONAUT
OTHER STUFF - HAS RECEIVED 21,453
SPEEDING TICKETS IN HER LIFETIME

HERE COMES SISTER SPEED!

Faster than a flash
She's a raging rocket
She's a white-hot wire
An electric socket
She's a lightning bolt
She's a rampant cheetah
Plot and plan a crime
And she will defeat you

Whizzing to the rescue
In your hour of need
Here comes Sister Speed!

Racing down the road
Tearing through the traffic
Sweeping to the scene
When you're in a panic
She's a whirring blur
Breaking all speed limits
100 metre gold
Guaranteed to win it

Zipping to the rescue
In your hour of need
Here comes Sister Speed!

There is no stopwatch
Quick enough to time her
When her molten core's
Welling up inside her
See that shooting star?
It can never match her
Want her autograph?
Then you'll have to catch her

Zooming to the rescue
In your hour of need
Here comes Sister Speed!

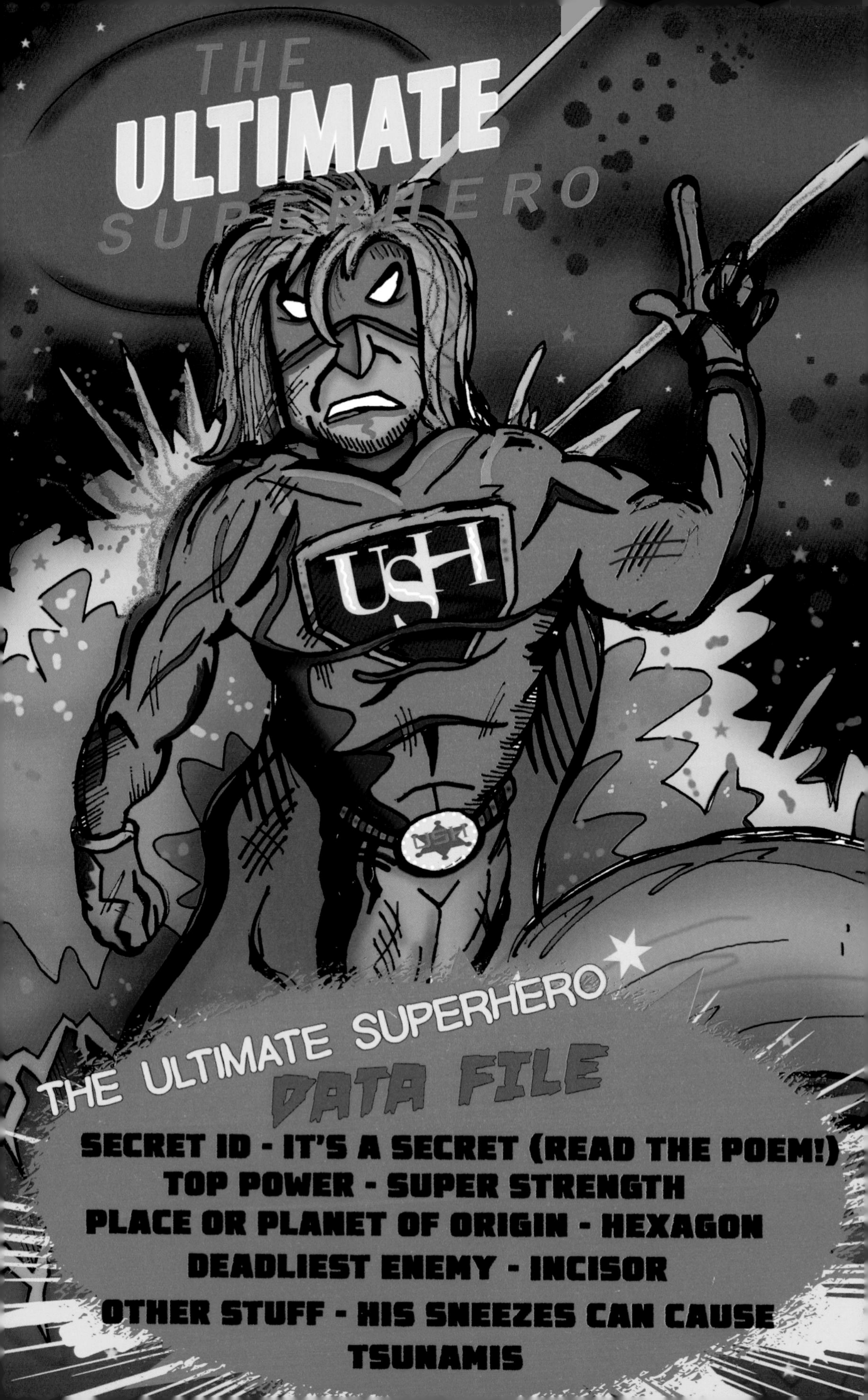
THE ULTIMATE SUPERHERO
USH
THE ULTIMATE SUPERHERO
DATA FILE
SECRET ID - IT'S A SECRET (READ THE POEM!)
TOP POWER - SUPER STRENGTH
PLACE OR PLANET OF ORIGIN - HEXAGON
DEADLIEST ENEMY - INCISOR
OTHER STUFF - HIS SNEEZES CAN CAUSE TSUNAMIS

THE ULTIMATE SUPERHERO

I'm the Ultimate Superhero
No job's too big or too small
When danger threatens our country
Or if your cat's stuck up a tree
It's me you'll want to call
I'm the Ultimate Superhero

If you're a bad guy then I'm your supreme test
My legs and arms are wider than your expanded chest
You'll recognise me by the golden U.S.H. on my vest
And like my fellow superheroes I've a cape to help me fly
If you shot, bashed, squashed or smashed me I'll never die
Though I don't suggest you try
I'll make my worst nemesis break down and cry
I'm the Ultimate Superhero

I'm indestructible, undefeatable, incorruptible
Totally unbeatable, ultra-intelligent, flabbergastingly fast
You'll not catch me in a plaster cast
I'll stop muggers who mug, robbers who rob
Kidnappers who kidnap, fighting crime is my job
I'm the Ultimate Superhero

Other superheroes are gentle pussycats next to me
Just beginners, novices, trainees
Absolutely nowhere in the reckoning
I'll spearhead the attack when danger's beckoning
I pack the most powerful of powerful punches
I start work at six and never stop for tea or lunches
Do you know who the pick of the superhero bunch is?
Me - I'm the Ultimate Superhero

I've got a secret identity like all superheroes do
Who am I? It's a secret so I'm not telling you
But rest assured I'll be there when I am needed
When the laws of this nation are no longer heeded
I'll be first in the queue to protect you
Beating supervillains is what I do
So you can sleep safely in your beds at night
You've no need to live in fear, no
Leave it to me to keep you free
I'm the Ultimate Superhero

NUMBER
1

GADGET MAN DATA FILE

Secret ID - Marius B Rain

Top Power - Cleverness

Place or Planet of Origin - Silicon Valley

Deadliest Enemy - Mister Gadget (his main competitor in the gadget market)

Other Stuff - Opens his shop even on Bank Holidays and gives discounts to pensioners

GADGET MAN

I've got gadgets that will help you
climb and drill into brick walls
I've got gadgets that will do things
that you thought impossible

I've got gadgets that will help you
run as quick as you can blink
I've got gadgets to enlarge you
and to also help you shrink

I've got gadgets that will help you
breathe in deepest darkest space
I've got gadgets that will help you
change your accent and your face

I've got gadgets that will help your
fingers fire flaming sparks
I've got gadgets that will help you
see broad daylight in the dark

I've got gadgets that will help you
turn into a telepath
I've got gadgets that will help you
be a genius at maths

I've got gadgets made with lasers
and the latest in high-tech
I've got gadgets wired to gadgets
no-one has invented yet

Want to beat that supervillain?
Then include me in your plans
Book yourself the next appointment -
come and meet the Gadget Man

SUPER SNIPPET
The author also considered
'MASK & BOOTS & BELT'
as this poem's title

CAPE & TIGHTS & PANTS
(OR HOW TO BECOME A SUPERHERO)

If your life adds up to zero
Cape & tights & pants
Why not be a superhero?
Cape & tights & pants

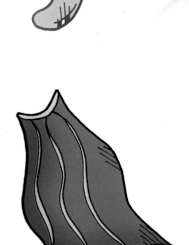

Grab yourself a special power
Cape & tights & pants
Save the planet every hour
Cape & tights & pants

Flying lessons - have to take them
Cape & tights & pants
Mega muscles - have to make them
Cape & tights & pants

Pick yourself a secret ID
Cape & tights & pants
Be a cop or run a library
Cape & tights & pants

Find yourself a supervillain
Cape & tights & pants
Always beat them, never kill them
Cape & tights & pants

Sound effects are very useful
Cape & tights & pants
Bash, crash, smash, bang, whack and splat too
Cape & tights & pants

Buy your clothes from Costume Central
Cape & tights & pants
Which bits are the most essential?
Cape & tights & pants

Say which bits are the most essential?
Cape & tights & pants
Cape & tights & pants
Cape & tights & pants

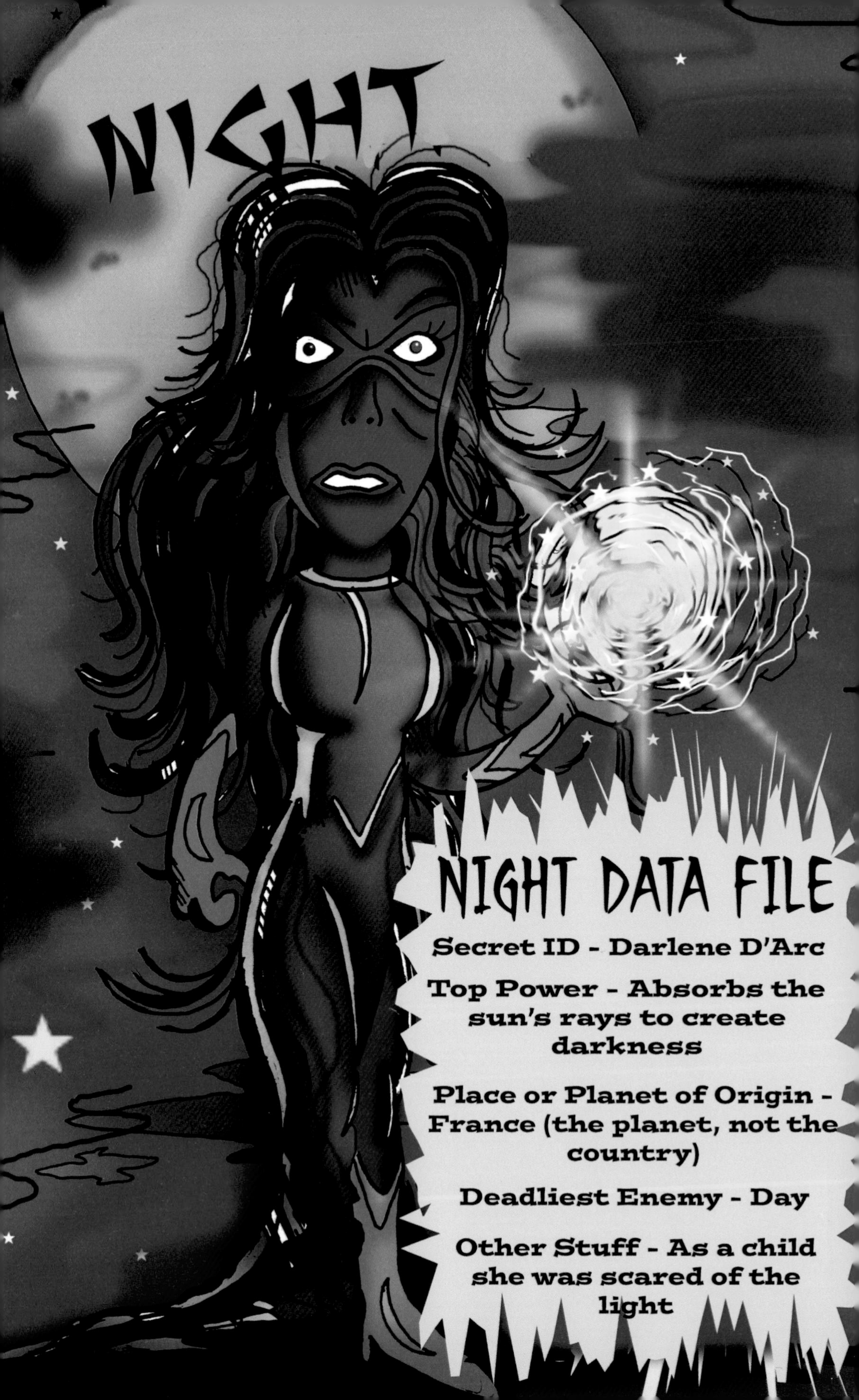
NIGHT
NIGHT DATA FILE
Secret ID - Darlene D'Arc
Top Power - Absorbs the sun's rays to create darkness
Place or Planet of Origin - France (the planet, not the country)
Deadliest Enemy - Day
Other Stuff - As a child she was scared of the light

NIGHT

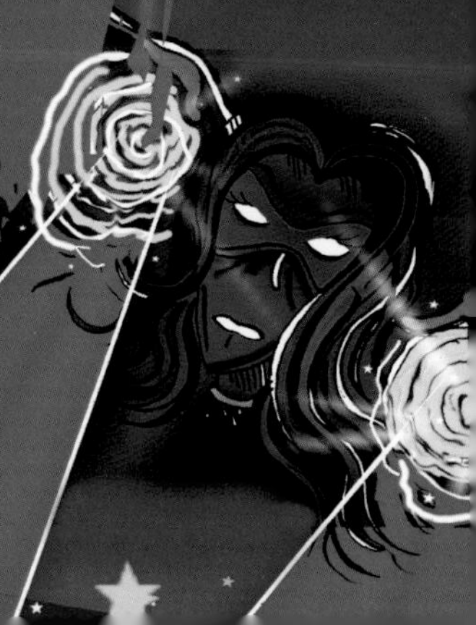

She is black
She is dark
She is awesome
She is stark

She'll dance with you, confound you
She will wrap her arms around you

She is brave
She is bold
She is magic
She is cold

She'll mesmerise, control you
Steal your mind and take your soul too

She is grim
She is grey
She's the opposite of Day

Is she hero?
Is she villain?
There's no simple way of telling
As she vanishes by light
She is Night

SHINE

SHINE DATA FILE

Secret ID – Keiko Kudo

Top Power – Dazzleness

Place or Planet of Origin – Tokyo

Deadliest Enemy – Samurai Strike

Other Stuff – Can recharge herself
on sunbeds

SHINE

When there's gleaming in your eye
And a beaming in the sky
When the whole world is fluorescent
With a glow of luminescence
Through the chaos it's the time
For Shine

Light electric that surrounds
Scorching grass upon the ground
Supervillains run for cover
She has brightness like no other
Now it has to be the time
For Shine

As a scintillating jewel
Burning never-ending fuel
Is she human is she creature?
Is she more a force of nature?
When there's danger it's the time
For Shine

There's no night there's only day
You'll conceal yourself in shade
Spreading solar radiation
Queen of all illumination
Where there's darkness it's the time
For Shine

SUPER SNIPPET
Superhero experts estimate that over 4350 sound
effects have been used in superhero comics and movies
since monitoring commenced in 1938

ONOMATOHEROES

Booooooom!
Solar Soldier tackles monster hoards upon the moon
Thumpppppp!
Mister Mighty Muscles saves a town from Deadly Doom
Woooooosh!
Purple Pigeon's soaring swiftly into darkened skies
Zzzzzzip!
Sister Speed sprints to the rescue
Did you see her gliding by?

Craaaaaack!
Now the Red Volcano wants to get in on the act
Baaaang!
Mistress Universe destroys an alien attack
Boiiiiiing!
Catapult fights robber gangs who plan a cunning raid
Splaaaaaat!
Orange Master catches crooks
With radioactive marmalade

Whippppppp!
Wild Witch ties up two bad guys with her gold lasso
Hiyaaaaaah!
Watch Karate Chicken wield his wacky, weird kung fu
Powwwwww!
Lady Lionheart defeats a villain with one punch
Brrrrrr!
Ice Cold Kid has vowed to save all humankind
In time for lunch

Here come the superheroes, so cover up your ears
Battling their enemies with onomatopoeia!

SUPER SNIPPET

RECENT STATISTICS SHOW THAT
SUPERVILLAINS BEAT SUPERHEROES
IN ONLY 0.0002% OF ALL BATTLES

THE SUPERVILLAIN'S VIEW

Life's not easy being a supervillain
Forever misunderstood
Beaten and bashed
Trounced and trashed
By those wretched superheroes who prefer to do good

Why can't they let me get the girl?
Why can't they let me conquer the world?
I might make it a far better place
Mind-controlling the whole human race
If only they'd give me a chance...

The media too are constantly on my back
Saying it's my fault for each random attack
Or bomb disappearing from a military base
Or alien invasion from outer space

When the ozone layer had a hole in
When the Bank of England's cash was stolen
They wanted a scapegoat so they blamed me
They wanted a fall guy so they named me
Life's not easy being a supervillain

Why can't I star in my own monthly comic
Featuring my adventures with my logo on it?
You'd read about the dastardly deeds I've done
Like when I siphoned the heat from the sun
Or when I built a gigantic glue gun
Being evil should be much more fun!

My expensive costume gets torn and tattered
Each week my body gets bruised and battered
My secret identity has been revealed
My invisible hideout is no longer concealed

I had a difficult childhood you see
But I'm not looking for sympathy
As defeat follows defeat
And my patience wears thin
Is there any way if just for one day
That you could allow me to win?
'Cause life's not easy being a supervillain

V. Str
out
A

Glue in
here
Construction
Glue
B

TOP
SECRET

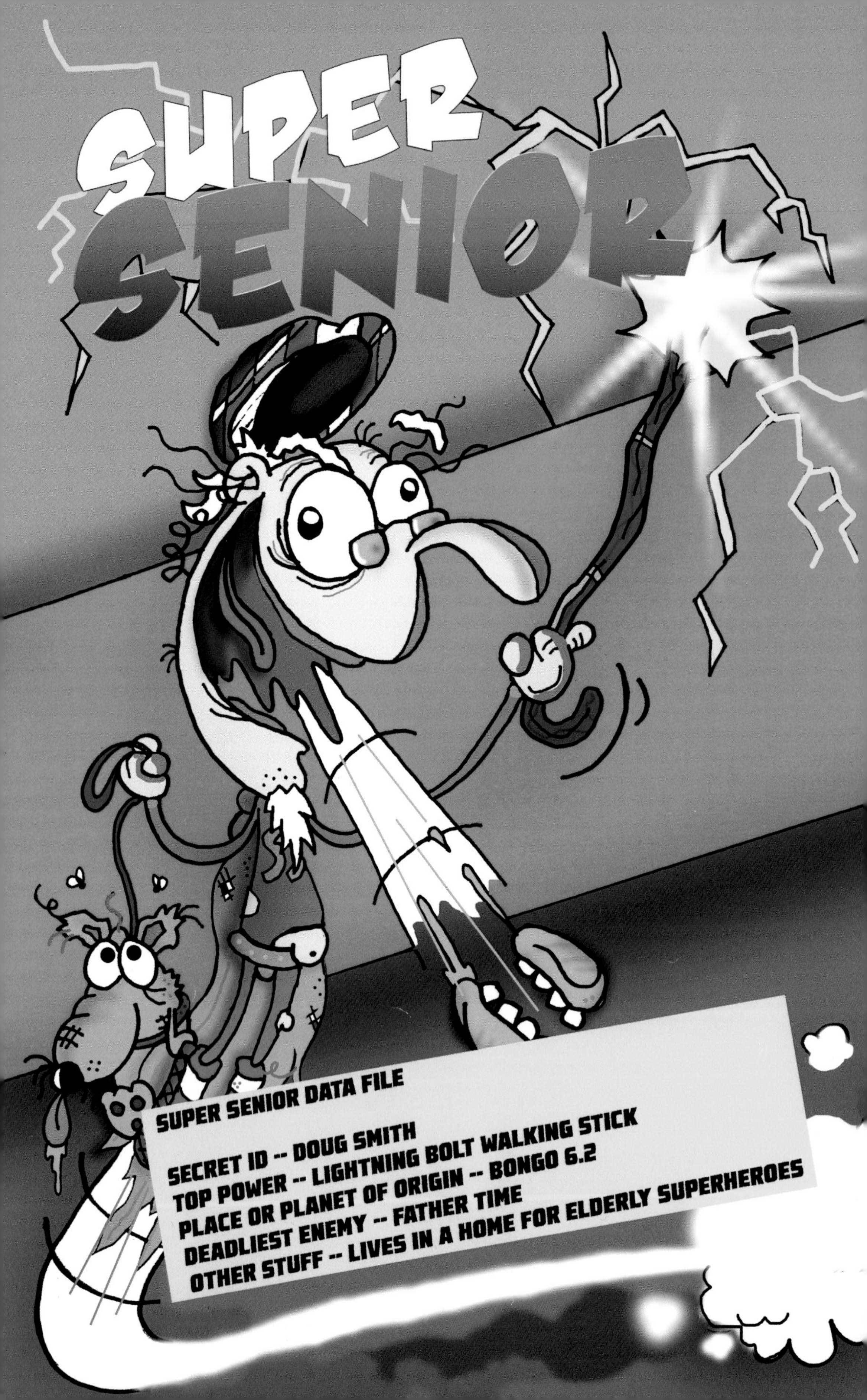
SUPER SENIOR
SUPER SENIOR DATA FILE
SECRET ID -- DOUG SMITH
TOP POWER -- LIGHTNING BOLT WALKING STICK
PLACE OR PLANET OF ORIGIN -- BONGO 6.2
DEADLIEST ENEMY -- FATHER TIME
OTHER STUFF -- LIVES IN A HOME FOR ELDERLY SUPERHEROES

SUPER SENIOR

His hair is grey and every day
A little more strength slips away
He's not so brave, he's not so bold
This superhero's rather old

He isn't in a healthy state
Now way beyond his sell-by date
His muscles sag, his body's thin
No villain's ever scared of him

His x-ray vision's not too good
He finds it hard to see through wood
His laser eyes are just a spark
That flicker dimly in the dark

To keep fit he might take a jog
Or choose to walk his ageing dog
'Cause pumping iron at the gym
Is far too strenuous for him

His super costume's frayed and worn
He wears it when he mows the lawn
For gardening takes up his time
Defeating weeds instead of crime

And if the weather's warm and dry
He zooms about up in the sky
A crowd will shout from on the ground
"How does that bloke still fly around?"

So though his younger days have gone
This pensioner fights on and on
Insisting that he is the best
To help you if you're in distress

The INVISIBLE Lady

The Invisible Lady Data File

Secret ID - Monica Clear
Top Power - Phases through solid objects
Place or Planet of Origin - The Selenic Galaxy
Deadliest Enemy - Diamondia
Other Stuff - On her own planet some people are invisible for life

The Invisible Lady

I'm going out with the Invisible Lady
I'm meeting her for a date
I'm going out with the Invisible Lady
She said she'd meet me at eight
But she's making me wait
She's one hour late
Though I couldn't find her
If I was standing behind her

I'm going out with the Invisible Lady
Though what she looks like I don't know
I'm going out with the Invisible Lady
I could so easily tread on her toe
Or leave without her when we go
To the cinema or to a show
It is quite apparent
She's totally transparent

I'm going out with the Invisible Lady
I walked right through her last night
I'm going out with the Invisible Lady
I can't see her though it's broad daylight
Like a polar bear on a background of white
She's out of my sight
The torture I've been through
'Cause my girlfriend's see-through

I'm going out with the Invisible Lady
Though we've never met face to face
I'm going out with the Invisible Lady
She could be standing in this very place
Though all you see is empty space
Don't say I'm a nutcase!
My woman's invisible - it's true
She just vanishes into the blue

I'm going out with the Invisible Lady
I'm still waiting here on my own
I'm going out with the Invisible Lady
Looks like one more evening alone
She's got no skin and bones
But she still could have phoned
I guess I'm not in her future plans
Perhaps she's run off - with the Invisible Man

CAPTAIN POLYSTYRENE

CAPTAIN POLYSTYRENE DATA FILE

Secret ID - Paul E Styrene
Top Power - None
Place or Planet of Origin - Clapham Common
Deadliest Enemy - Colonel Glass
Other Stuff - Owns a pet parrot called Polly Styrene

this way up

CAPTAIN POLYSTYRENE

There's a hero who's unusual
And some say most peculiar
Who's not composed of silver, steel or rock
He looks ready to expire
Melts away in any fire
He's Captain Polystyrene
And he's not much cop

Weedy as a tiny feather
Watch him crumble in bad weather
Never giving people confidence at all
There's nobody who is lighter
There's nobody who is whiter
He's Captain Polystyrene
And he's so uncool

He may break up during battle
Even when in fights with cattle
He is weaker than a milky cup of tea
With a face that's full of pimples
And a body full of dimples
He's Captain Polystyrene
A catastrophe

No-one cares when he's attacking
Once this guy was used in packing
He's constructed from some old leftover scraps
Flexing muscles far too little
He's a polymer who's brittle
He's Captain Polystyrene
Quite a useless chap

Yes he's really unfantastic
Strictly speaking he's a plastic
And his enemy's the fragile Colonel Glass
With frail frames they both are lumbered
I think that their days are numbered
He's Captain Polystyrene
You should call him last

SUPER SNIPPET

Research, conducted in the Selenic Galaxy in 2012, revealed that superheroes who do not wear masks are far more confident and much happier than those who do

UNDERNEATH THE MASK

Underneath the mask
I'm a regular guy
Underneath the mask
I'm quiet and shy
Underneath the mask
I'm human too
Underneath the mask
I'm just like you

I've a life that's ordinary
I go shopping and watch telly

Underneath the mask
I'm much more humble
Underneath the mask
I'm vulnerable
Underneath the mask
I'm not well-known
Underneath the mask
I'm all alone

I get nervous when I'm flying
When I fight I'm scared of dying

Underneath the mask
I'm not so strong
Underneath the mask
My powers have gone
Underneath the mask
Is a different man
Underneath the mask
Who I really am

Nobody will recognise me
Hidden by my secret ID
There's no superhero to see.
Underneath the mask

MR ELASTIC DATA FILE
Secret ID - Ron E Raser
Top Power - Streeeeeeeeeetchability
Place or Planet of Origin - Rubberworld
Deadliest Enemy - Doc Scissors
Other Stuff - Regularly ties himself in knots so has to call emergency
services

Mr Elastic

I stretch to the Moon, I stretch to the stars
To Jupiter, Saturn and way beyond Mars
I stretch my muscles to make myself stronger
In the whole wide world there's nobody longer
I stretch into the garden, down the hall and up the stairs
I stretch under rugs, carpets, tables and chairs
I've been like this since I was created
I live my life forever elongated

I'm a friendly, bendy, never-ending man
Mr Elastic that's who I am

I stretch down the baker's to buy a loaf of bread
I'll need a 50-foot grave to bury me in when I'm dead
I love to see the shock on strangers' faces
When I don't kneel down to tie my shoelaces
I stretch up high, I stretch wide and low
I stretch my head, shoulders, knees and toes
(I can even stretch my nose)
I stretch up the ladder to the window cleaner
And quickly contract like a cool concertina

I'm a friendly, bendy, never-ending man
Mr Elastic that's who I am

I stretch to Mount Everest, skyscrapers and aeroplanes
Through manhole cover cracks, along sewers and drains
From a sitting down position I mend broken lights
You'll not find a tape measure half my height
I stretch to the bottom, I reach the top
I stretch to King's Cross Station and my local bus stop
People say "Be careful or you might snap"
I say "Don't dismay, I'm OK, I'm a stretchable chap"

I'm a friendly, bendy, never-ending man
Mr Elastic that's who I am

SUPER SNIPPET

NUMBER OF TELEPHONE BOXES, EARTH 1980: TOO MANY TO COUNT

NUMBER OF TELEPHONE BOXES, EARTH 2080: ZERO

THE LAST TELEPHONE BOX

You've vanished from our cities
And disappeared from towns
So where's a hero s'posed to change
When trouble's going down?

I used to use you daily
Strip off my outer clothes
To then reveal the costume
That all fans of mine will know

I loved your cuboid structure
Your squarish shiny glass
Now I undress in alleyways
Or find an underpass

There were so many of you
In high streets and in malls
You kept my secret ID safe
While I put crooks in jails

I know progress must happen
We have to turn that page
But when the mobile phone was born
It killed your Golden Age

Though I'm a man who's super
Unhurt by guns or rocks
My heart inside felt heavy pain
As they removed...the last telephone box

terrific tot

TERRIFIC TOT DATA FILE

Secret ID – Timmy Jones
Top Power – Ear-splitting screams
Place or Planet of Origin – Gooseberry bush, Epping Forest
Deadliest Enemy – Teen Terrible
Other Stuff – Often stops mid-battle for nappy change

terrific tot

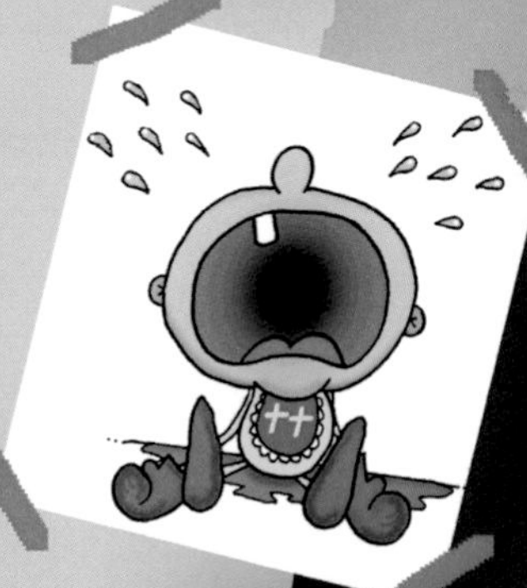

He's a hero in a nappy
But don't let that put you off
He can tackle twenty rhinos
He can handle rough and tough
Though he nearly is a newborn
And still peeing in a pot
He's the baby who can save me
Shout his name
Terrific Tot!

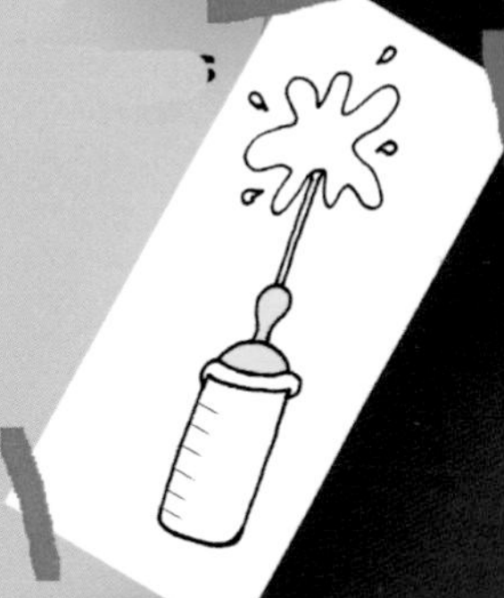

Special milk gives him his power
Special biscuits give him speed
Holds his rattle during battle
Always back for his next feed
Though he goo-goos and he gaa-gaas
And his nose is dripping snot
He's the one the needy run to
Shout his name
Terrific Tot!

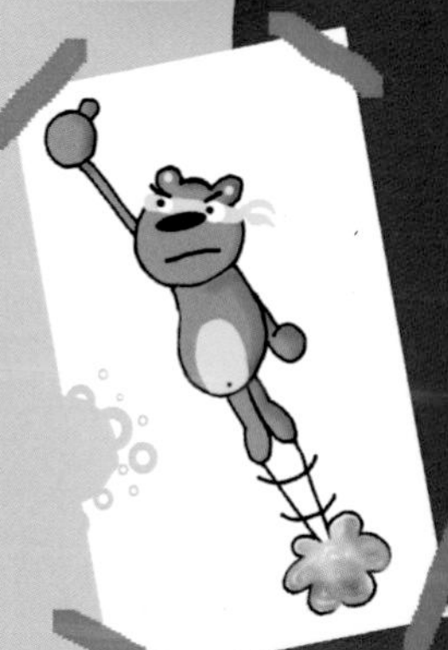

Spot him in his bib of spandex
Matching mittens on his hands
Grabbing kids from burning buildings
Crushing evil where it stands
Though he's tiny, sometimes whiny
And spends nighttimes in a cot
He's a cutie dressed in booties
Shout his name
Terrific Tot!

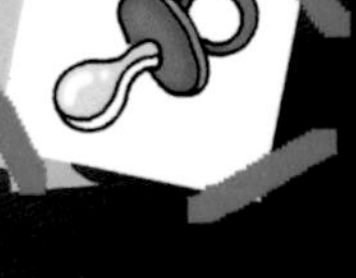

He's attending kindergarten
Missing lessons to fight crime
While he's cuddling his teddy
Ending evil every time
Though he's sucking on his dummy
And his mum still wipes his bot
He's the best to stage a rescue
Shout his name
Terrific Tot!

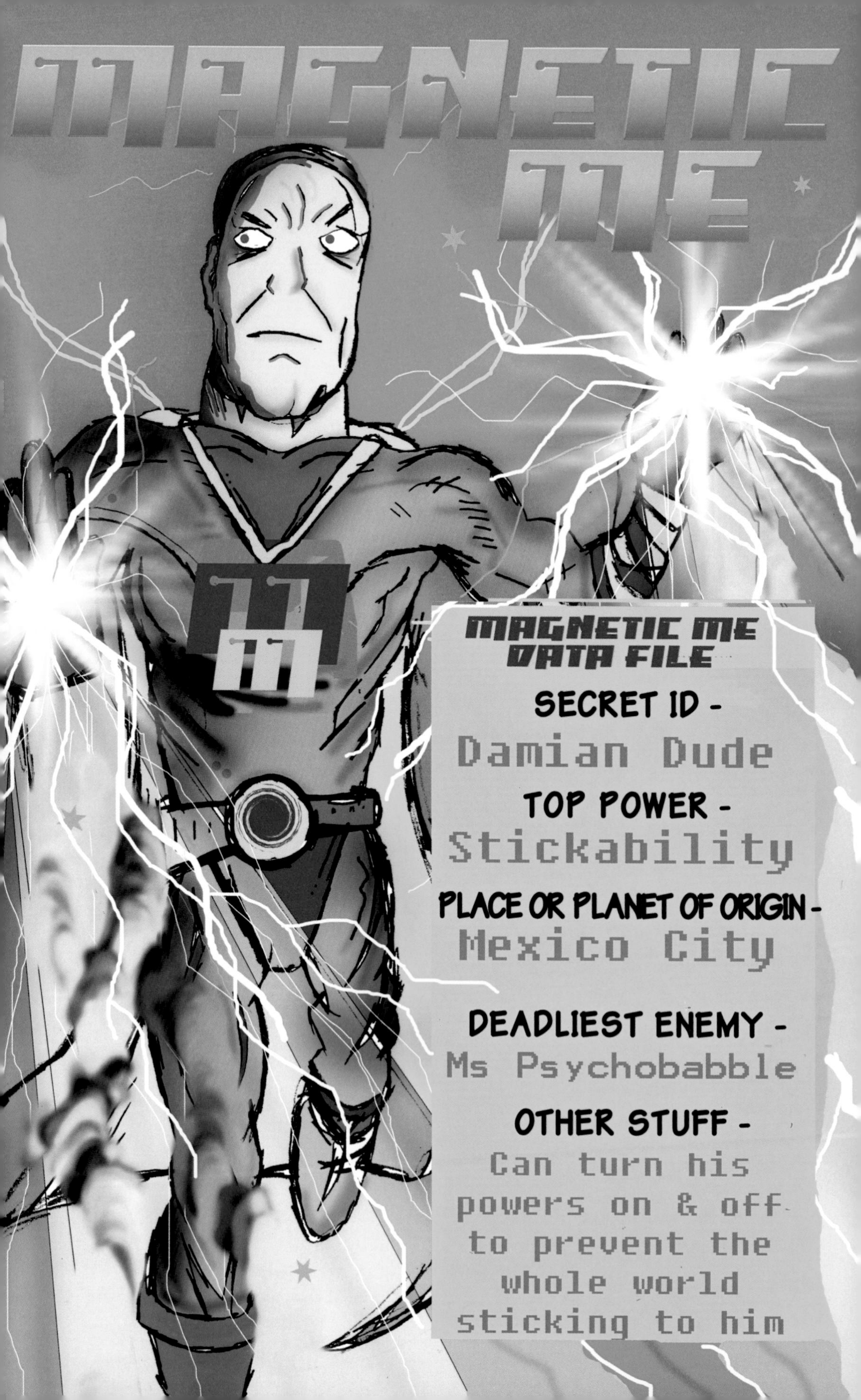
MAGNETIC ME
MAGNETIC ME DATA FILE
SECRET ID -
Damian Dude
TOP POWER -
Stickability
PLACE OR PLANET OF ORIGIN -
Mexico City
DEADLIEST ENEMY -
Ms Psychobabble
OTHER STUFF -
Can turn his powers on & off to prevent the whole world sticking to him

MAGNETIC ME

Magnetic Me
Magnetic Me

Anything and everything sticks to me
Carpets, cars, books, TVs
Pencils, pens and bumblebees
Tables, trousers, front door keys
Newspapers and DVDs

Magnetic Me
Magnetic Me

It happens totally naturally
I've an instant connectivity
Defying the laws of gravity
Come near you'll adhere instantly

Magnetic Me
Magnetic Me

Scientists they all agree
I've a very unusual biology
I'm the gluiest person in history
I'm a gent like cement you can't shake free

Magnetic Me
Magnetic Me

More power than a magnet factory
Shake hands you'll be stuck by the count of three
One look you'll be hooked like a fish in the sea
I've a magnetic personality

Magnetic Me
Magnetic Me

I'm an
M.A.G.
N.E.T.
What's my name?
Magnetic Me!

Supermum Data File

Secret ID - ....(insert your Mum's name)
Top Power - Multitasking
Place or Planet of Origin - Earth
Deadliest Enemy - Housework
Other Stuff - Regularly tops the superhero popularity charts

SUPERMUM

She's a super Supermum
As amazing as they come, she'll do anything for us
Without a moan, without a fuss
Cooks our dinner, gets us dressed
Always clears up all our mess
Never has a time to rest, and she's got a day job too
Who's the captain of our crew?
Super Supermum

She is top, does the supermarket shop
Polishes our shoes, wipes our noses
Disinfects the loo, buys us clotheses
And apart from hugs and kisses never asks for anything back
Whatever she does she's got the knack
When we're naughty she puts us back on track
Who's the leader of our pack?
Super Supermum

Mrs Everywhere
Combing our hair, driving us to school
Still she's smiling, the Queen of Cool
Although she never gets paid at all for her labours
Next she's running errands for elderly neighbours
Who will forever do you favours?
Super Supermum

Washing up, tidying up
Sewing up, drying up, ironing, vacuuming
Cleaning, cleaning, cleaning, cleaning
Making beds, darning socks
And she rarely puts her feet up until it's nine o'clock
But she still lets us watch what we want to watch
On the box
Super Supermum

Her day's non-stop
She carries on while others would drop
Whatever needs doing she does the lot
And more
Without her we couldn't cope for sure
She's our own superhero
Though she has no superpowers, just kindness
And thoughtfulness, for hours and hours
I really think Dad should buy her more flowers
Who needs superheroes stronger than steel
When they're pretend but our Mum's real?
Super Supermum

SUPER SNIPPET

The IUS (International Union of Superheroes) has set up a 24-hour helpline for reporting findings of any stolen powers or supervillains who have stolen them: 0880 6714 4222

Somebody Stole My Powers

My lasers won't burn and my muscles won't lift
I cannot fly high or punch with a fist
As a superhero I no longer exist
I'm a glass of milk gone sour
Since somebody stole my powers

I can't move fast 'cause my legs won't run
I'm missing the plug from my water gun
From a perfect ten I'm down to a one
The villains all laugh not cower
Since somebody stole my powers

I was king of the world till disaster struck
Now I can't pick up a toy pickup truck
I swim and get overtaken by ducks
I'm weedier than a dead flower
Since somebody stole my powers

I can't teleport through the thinnest wall
With no strength to burst a small plastic ball
I was beaten up in a nursery school
I wobble like a crumbling tower
Since somebody stole my powers

My skin is pierced by the bluntest pin
When I battle bad guys there's no way to win
So you might as well throw me in your bin
I'm not the hero of the hour
Since somebody stole my powers

PROFESSOR BAD

PROFESSOR BAD DATA FILE

Secret ID - Johan Bad
Top Power - Incredible Kindness
Place or Planet of Origin - Opposite 3
Deadliest Enemy - Professor Good
(who is actually bad)
Other stuff - Currently attending a
positive thinking course

PROFESSOR BAD

About a superhero born with an unfortunate last name!

I'm Professor Bad
But I'm actually good
A superhero misunderstood
Not a Sheriff of Nottingham
More a Robin Hood

Proving you can't tell a book by its cover
If I could pick a surname I'd choose any other
This mess is the fault of my father and mother
Really, I'm not bad at all

I help young children cross busy streets
I always offer old ladies my seat
The nicest person you ever could meet
Though as I fight for freedom in the universe
My negative title weighs me down like a curse

Why isn't there a halo above me
As people out there clearly love me?
Honestly, I'm not bad at all

Yet I'm stuck with this problem
For the rest of my life
Mrs Bad is too (yes, she's my wife)
Nobody I rescue is ever impressed
To see the word 'Bad' written on my chest
I'd even take a lie detector test
To show you I'm not bad at all

So don't say to me, "What's in a name?"
I'd reply, "A great deal in this superhero game"
I repeat it again and again and again
Why can't you cement it into your brain
That villains and me are not the same?
I'm Professor Bad, kind, considerate, cool
If you think me evil then you've been fooled
It's safe to let me into your home or school
Because I'm good not bad at all

MICRO GIRL

DATA FILE

SECRET ID - DOLLY DOT
TOP POWER - SMALLNESS
PLACE OR PLANET OF ORIGIN - MICRONOVIA
DEADLIEST ENEMY - ANYONE WITH BIG FEET
OTHER STUFF - EMBARRASSINGLY, HER COSTUME
SOMETIMES DOES NOT SHRINK WITH HER

MICRO GIRL

She's Micro Girl
Smaller than an ant
You try and find her but I bet you can't
She soars through the skyways
On silky wings
Zapping supervillains
With sonic stings
Electric blue cape
Titanium suit
Don't underestimate her because she's cute

She's Micro Girl
Like a tiny spot
Concealing herself beneath a full stop
To her they're "green boulders"
To us they're "peas"
To her they're "huge monsters"
To us they're "fleas"
Though minuscule
She's extremely strong
With a single punch she can topple King Kong

She's Micro Girl
Just a teeny spec
The coolest creation you've ever met
When behind a breadcrumb
She's out of sight
When next to an atom
She's still a mite
Who's saving the day
And giving us hope?
The mini heroine from the microscope

MEGA SLUG

Mega Slug DATA FILE

Secret ID – Graham Grimy

Top Power – Shoots poisonous slime

Place or Planet of Origin –
Urth (not to be confused with Earth)

Deadliest Enemy – Kid Slug Pellet

Other Stuff – Officially the slowest superhero ever

MEGA SLUG

When I was bitten by a radioactive slug
I thought I'd become a superhero
Though I'm not the type to give villains a fright
'Cause am I the one who they would fear? No!

If there's a bank job in the town today
I'll arrive at the scene next week
Slowly I'll slide after robbers and crooks
Who've long since escaped down the street

Super costumes I've worn – they never fit me
I'm such a short cylindrical shape
This secondhand one I wear is too long
Presented to me by Super Snake

At fighting I'll never make Heavyweight Champ
With no fists for a knockout punch
So while I should be bashing them baddies
I might be chewing through your salad lunch

But if you're an evil sort I'll do my best
To tackle you and then beat you
'If you can't face my slime then don't do the crime'
Will be my battle cry as I defeat you!

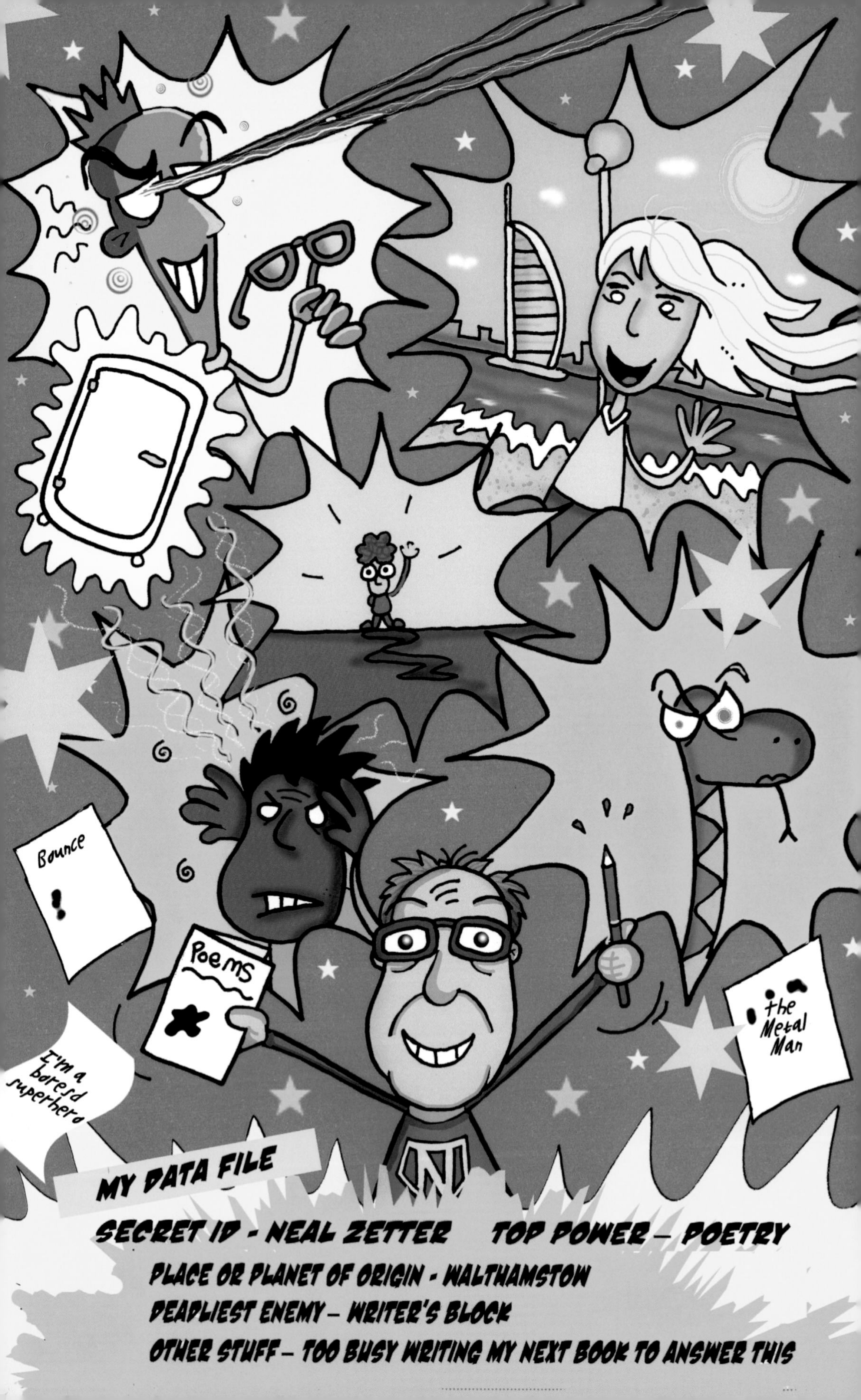

Bounce
Poems
I'm a bored superhero
the Metal Man

MY DATA FILE

SECRET ID – NEAL ZETTER

TOP POWER – POETRY

PLACE OR PLANET OF ORIGIN – WALTHAMSTOW

DEADLIEST ENEMY – WRITER'S BLOCK

OTHER STUFF – TOO BUSY WRITING MY NEXT BOOK TO ANSWER THIS

My Superpower...

My mate Max has laser vision
Melting metal with perfect precision
Browning toast, and the Sunday roast
Who has his own show on television?
My mate Max who has laser vision

My cousin Kate can teleport
Changing location with a single thought
In the blink of an eye, England to Dubai
Who moves from country to country without a passport?
My cousin Kate who can teleport

My buddy Bill can shrink to ant-size
When he does you can never fail to be surprised
Though possessing human strength
At one millimetre in length
Who still has to be wary of hungry flies?
My buddy Bill who can shrink to ant-size

My pal Pete is telekinetic
He can move any object by looking at it
Shifting the fridge, lifting a bridge
Who do all the girls call totally terrific?
My pal Pete who is telekinetic

My sister Sara can change her shape
Yesterday an octopus, today an ape
Often hard to recognise
The queen of disguise
Who morphs from a camel into a snake?
My sister Sara who can change her shape

But I can't turn invisible, run extra-fast or fly
As a poet I thought "I'm just an ordinary guy"
Then I saw I could inspire, I could engage
I could make people listen, read and turn over a page
Unlock creativity, spark imagination
Master the skill of communication

So if YOU want a superpower too
Whether you're a girl or guy
Get typing, get writing
And give poetry a try

Micro
Girl

Mega
slug

BOUNCE

BOUNCE DATA FILE

SECRET ID - Roland Ball   **TOP POWER** - Indestructibility
PLACE OR PLANET OF ORIGIN - Boinggg
DEADLIEST ENEMY - Hopscotch
OTHER STUFF - Has been used as the football in two World Cup Finals

BOUNCE

There's a man you can message
If you're ever in trouble
Body shape of a football
Or a massive soap bubble

Wears a costume of plastic
And a skin made of rubber
What a strange superhero
So unlike any other

He can bounce on the pavement
He can bounce off big buildings
He can bounce 'cross the ocean
He can splat supervillains

He can bounce over rooftops
He can bounce 'cross the blue sky
He can bounce along train tracks
He can flatten the bad guys

Such a cool Humpty Dumpty
With a trampoline tummy
Not a one you should mess with
Kangaroo mixed with bunny

Some have tried hard to burst him
Some have tried hard to pop him
But once Bounce starts his bouncing
There's no way they can stop him

BORED SUPERHERO DATA FILE

SECRET ID - HENRY (SECOND NAME UNKNOWN)
TOP POWER - EXCELLENT AT CROSSWORD PUZZLES
PLACE OR PLANET OF ORIGIN - ZZZZZZ
DEADLIEST ENEMY - HIMSELF
OTHER STUFF - HOPES TO TAKE UP GOLF SOON

BORED SUPERHERO

I'm a bored superhero
With nothing left to do
I've saved the Earth a hundred times
And distant planets too
Defeated every villain
And foiled their evil plans
No longer called to action
I'm not a busy man

I'm a bored superhero
Have you a job for me?
I'll help grannies crossing roads
Or rescue cats from trees
I'd rather face grave danger
And flex my muscles tight
Show off my mighty powers
Beat baddies in a fight

I'm a bored superhero
Now wearing normal clothes
With costume packed inside a box
I'm just another Joe
Nobody ever knows me
When I stroll into town
But I've made it a safer place
There's no crime to be found

I'm a bored superhero
So hire me if you like
I'll clean your house at triple speed
Or trace your stolen bike
Perform at children's parties
Or walk your dog for you
I'm a bored superhero
With nothing left to do

YAWN!

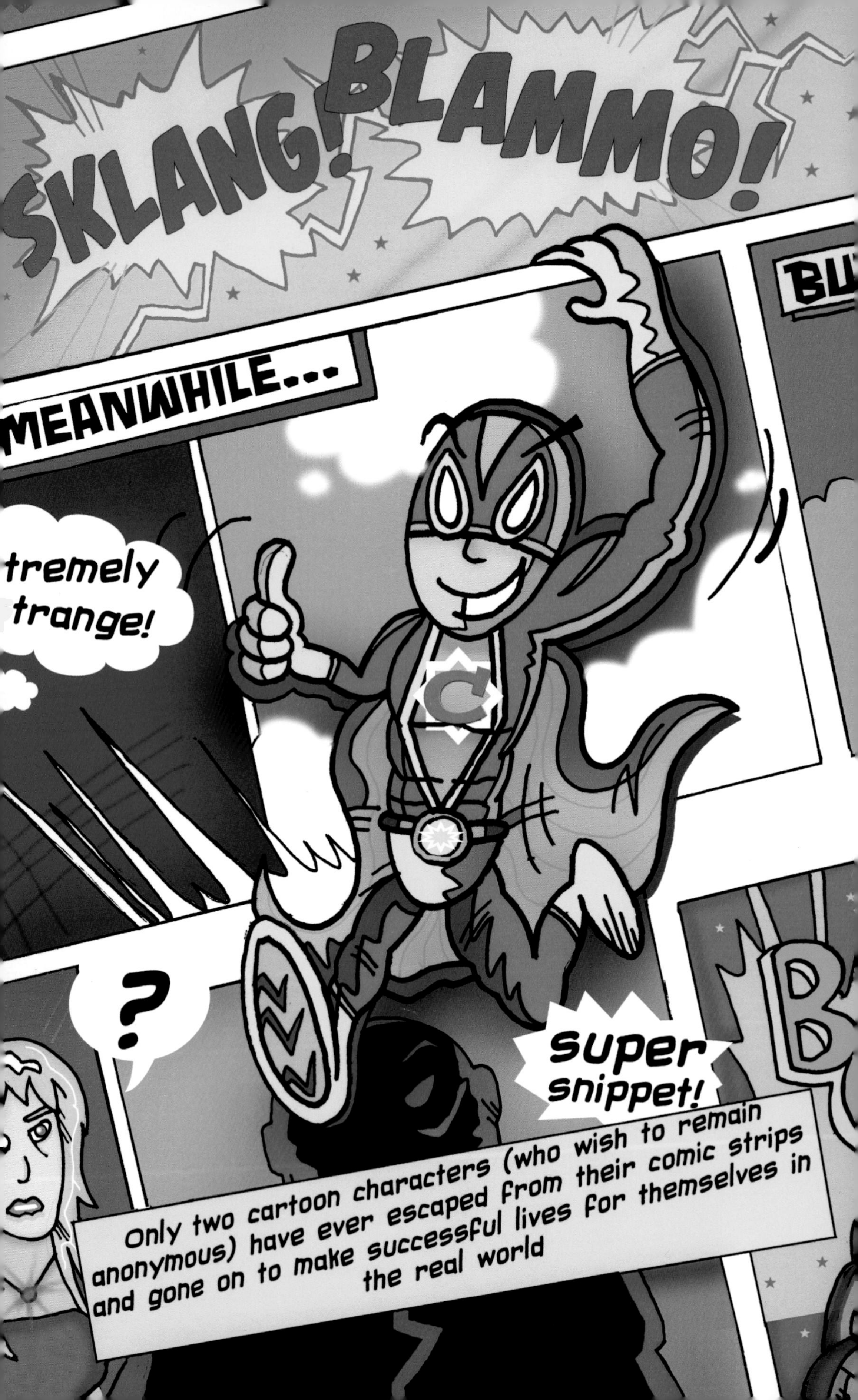
SKLANG!
BLAMMO!
MEANWHILE...
?
super snippet!
Only two cartoon characters (who wish to remain anonymous) have ever escaped from their comic strips and gone on to make successful lives for themselves in the real world

BORN A CARTOON

I was born a cartoon
Sitting on this very page
Feeling colourful and cool
Wacky, weird, extremely strange
I'm a 2D animation
From someone's imagination

It's an odd existence
Living in a world that's flat
With my home inside a frame
That's edged in white or black
Still I'm starring in this feature
Though I'm only just a picture

Titles rest above me
And an advert to my right
While in panels underneath
You'll find me in a fight
As a hero I'm no stranger
When it comes to facing danger

If I was a human
I'd jump from this comic strip
Buy a house and meet a wife
Then travel quite a bit
It's a dream it's my ambition
To be fact instead of fiction

But I remain a cartoon
Grab my mag and have a read
I will follow from behind
And let my artist lead
I am his unique creation
He made me an illustration

Now my story's ended
Please don't throw me in your bin
Store me somewhere safe and sound
So we can meet again
Or perhaps if you prefer to
Why not purchase next month's issue?

SUPER SNIPPET

The latest count has revealed that there are over 3127* superheroes in the universe (*including all parallel worlds).
Experts are currently compiling estimates of known supervillains

The skies are clogged and crowded
The costume shops sold out
Long underwear's in fashion
Too many superheroes about

Fierce battles raging daily
And fights on every street
Each time I turn a corner
There's another hero to meet

They all have their own fan clubs
They all have their own style
Are beautiful or handsome
And in seconds can run a mile

Their names I mix and muddle
Who's who I never know
I think they'd stretch to Saturn
If laid in line from head to toe

Each one has their own comic
Appears in their own book
Or features in a movie
Super types wherever I look

The best names have been taken
No powers now are new
But with too many supervillains about also...
We need all those superheroes too

SUPER SNIPPET

ONLY 2% OF ALL STORIES FEATURING CLIFFHANGER ENDINGS HAVE ACTUALLY INVOLVED A CLIFF OR SOMEBODY HANGING FROM IT...

Everyone Loves a Cliffhanger...

Will our hero make it just in time
To defuse a bomb or prevent a crime?
Will he stop that tank
Heading for the bank?
Everyone loves a cliffhanger

Will he save those children in distress?
Will he hold out firm or will he confess?
Will the plot be foiled?
Will he boil in oil?
Everyone loves a cliffhanger

Will he win the war but then lose the girl?
Live a life marooned on a distant world?
Will he slow the truck
Or press "self-destruct"?
Everyone loves a cliffhanger

Will his secret ID be revealed?
Will his nemesis have him cruelly killed?
Will he teleport
Or will he be caught?
Everyone loves a cliffhanger

Will he sink in quicksand like a stone?
Stay stuck in a cell locked away alone?
Will he spring the trap?
Will his frayed rope snap?
Everyone loves a cliffhanger

Will Professor Madd amputate his brain?
Will the antidote help him live again?
Will he break the spell?
I'm not allowed to tell
'Cause everyone loves a cliffhanger

ON

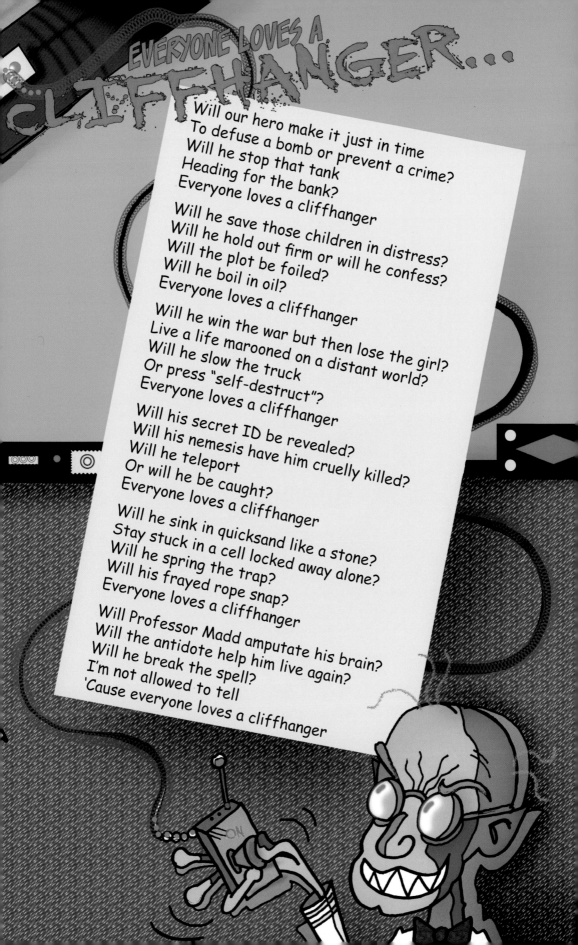

A VINTAGE COVER FROM THE VAULTS...

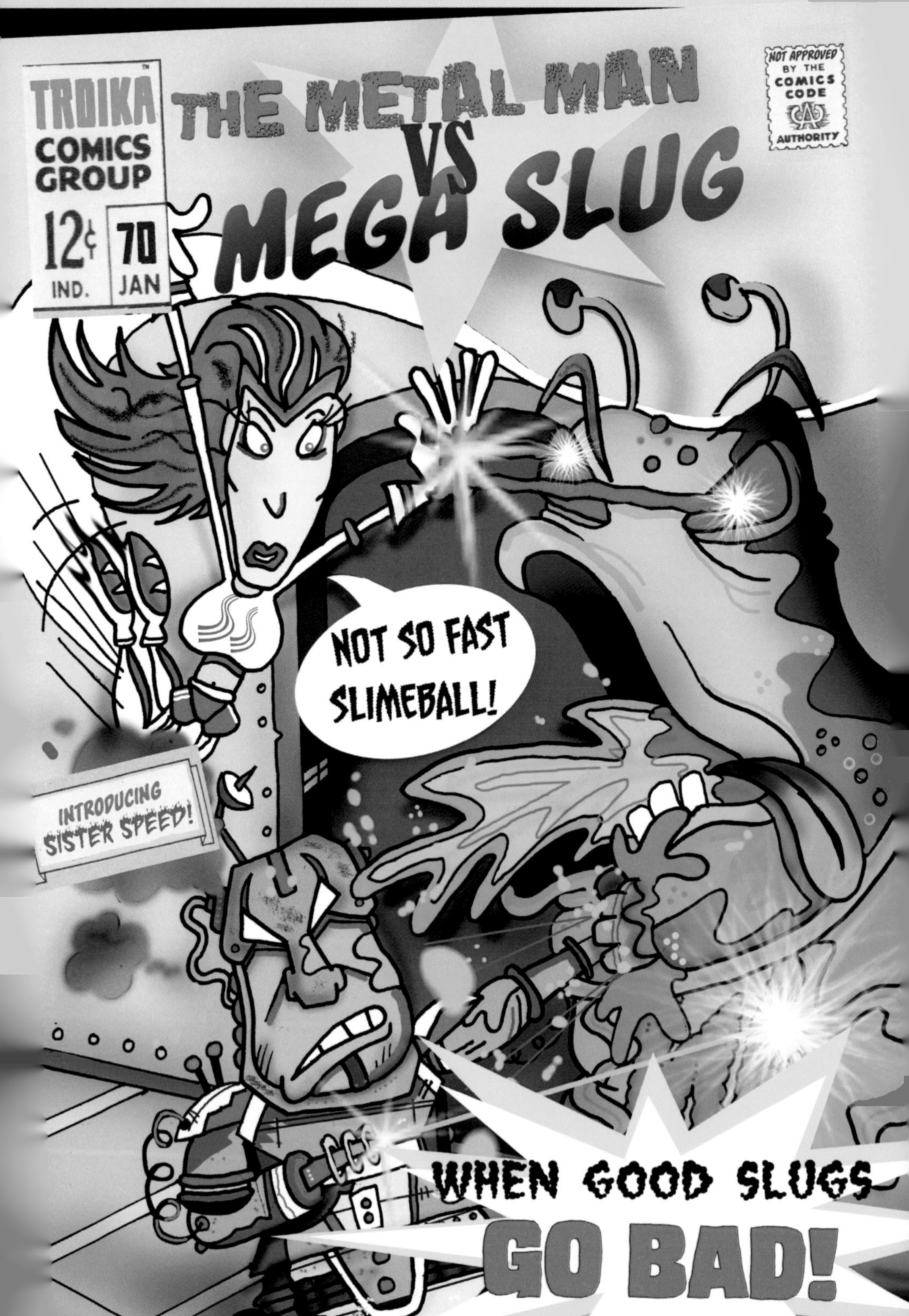
TROIKA COMICS GROUP
12¢ IND.
70 JAN
THE METAL MAN VS MEGA SLUG
NOT APPROVED BY THE COMICS CODE AUTHORITY
NOT SO FAST SLIMEBALL!
INTRODUCING SISTER SPEED!
WHEN GOOD SLUGS GO BAD!
NEAL ZETTER story CHRIS WHITE pencils NILES ZOTTER inks KEVIN BLACK lettering MARTIN WEST editor

DESIGN YOUR OWN SUPERHERO!

#herecometheheroes

draw face, hair & mask!

add gadgets!

every hero needs a symbol!

fill in the facts!

colour the costume!

.... **DATA FILE**

Secret ID:
Top Power -
Place or Planet of Origin-
Deadliest Enemy -
Other Stuff -

About the author

Secret ID: Neal Zetter
Top power: Poetry
Deadliest enemy: Writer's Block

Neal is a London-based comedy performance poet, author and entertainer with a huge following in schools. He has been using poetry writing and performance to develop literacy, confidence, self-expression, creativity and presentation skills in 3 to 103 year olds for over twenty years and his book, **Bees in My Bananas**, won the 2015 Wishing Shelf Independent Book Award. As well as schools, Neal has performed at comedy and poetry clubs, theatres, pubs, music venues, and the Royal Festival Hall. He lives in east London.

See **www.cccpworkshops.co.uk**
for information about Neal's work.

About the illustrator

Chris White keeps his Top Power secret but we know he's deadly with his pencil as he's also the incredible illustrator of **Bees in My Bananas, Odd Socks!** and **SSSSNAP! Mister Shark**. He is also a writer and poet who has created several popular characters including **Bitey the Veggie Vampire**. Chris has featured on radio and TV and travelled around the world bringing his cartoon and rhyme roadshows alive for lots of people.

See **www.veggievampire.com**
for information about Chris's work

More poems to enjoy by Neal Zetter

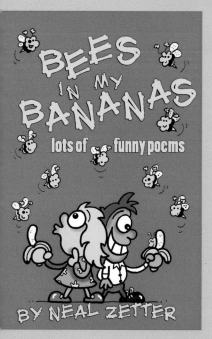

Enter the wacky wordy world of **Bees in my Bananas** and we promise you will be hooked. In these fun-packed, entertaining pages you will discover nearly fifty hilarious comedy odes tackling subjects of major importance: chocoholics, sumo wrestlers, sneezing, custard, puddles, itches, exploding underwear, superheroes, why you should never eat a whole elephant sandwich and heaps more too.

Your life will never be the same again!

Another original collection of comedy poems, **It's Not Fine to Sit on a Porcupine**, will make you tingle with excitement! It's a crazy rhyming romp through topics as weird as a bored superhero, an angry shopping trolley, a mammoth on the underground and even the world's worst toilet!

One of BookTrust's 20 favourite children's poetry books.

An amusingly illustrated collection of humorous poems from an award-winning performance poet, which covers a wide range of funny and interesting subjects' BookTrust

Rappy, happy poetic magic ... perfect for entertaining school classes or to be enjoyed by all the family at home' Pam Norfolk, Lancashire Evening Post

My First Performance Poetry Books

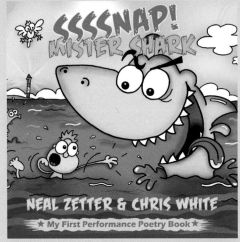

SSSSNAP! 'Mister Shark, don't eat me up!'

An irresistible first performance poetry book
encouraging readers to yell and clap their hands to
SSSSTOP Mister Shark every time he tries to have a nibble.
Impossible not to join in with this
SSSSUPER interactive poem's simple actions.

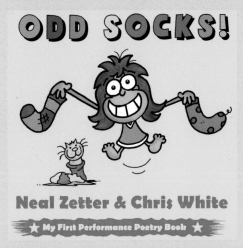

'Odd socks are all I ever wear,
I cannot make a matching pair.'

Sounds familiar? In this first performance poetry book
readers and listeners will enjoy calling out rhyming words and
performing simple actions to create a lively, interactive poem.

**Eye-catchingly colourful illustrations make these two books
a perfect introduction to rhythm and rhyme.**